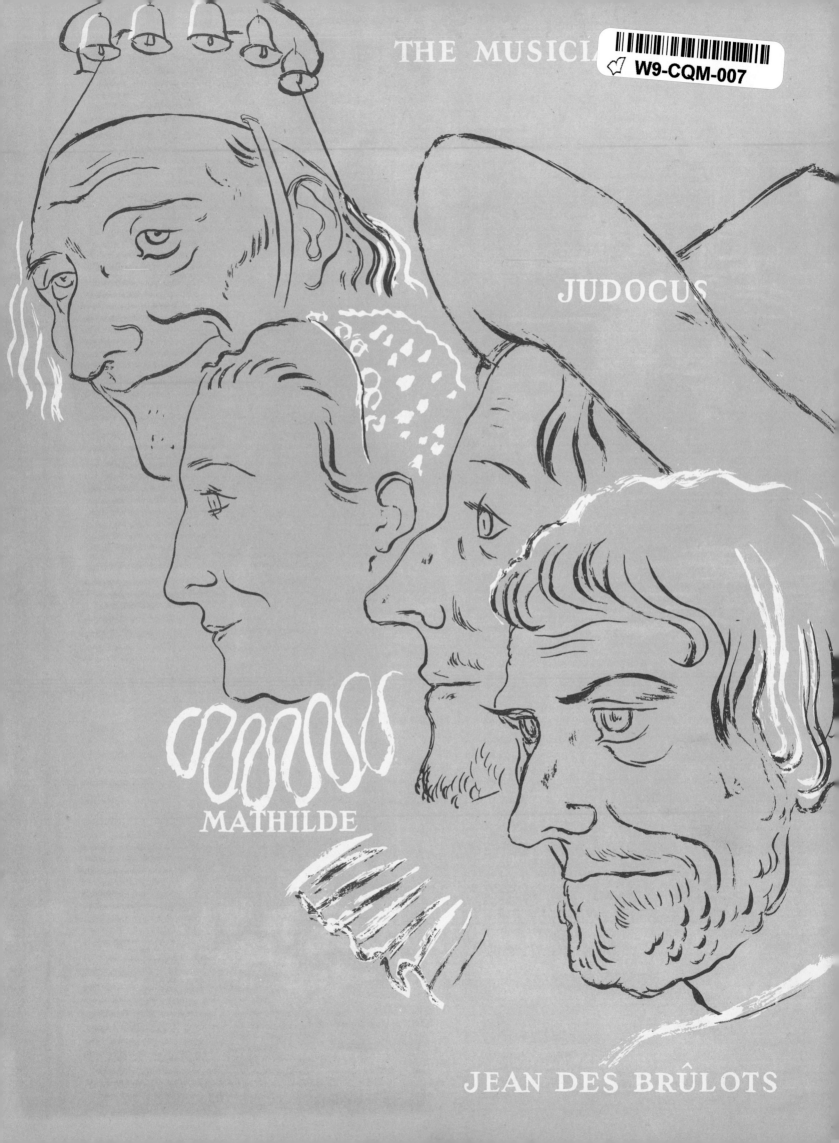

THE MUSICIA

JUDOCUS

MATHILDE

JEAN DES BRÛLOTS

MADELEINE LEY

The Enchanted Eve

Illustrated by EDY LEGRAND

HOWELL, SOSKIN,
PUBLISHERS, INC.

I

THE STEEPLES WERE ALL TURNING PINK. Judocus, the painter, had gone outside the city, carrying his little paralyzed girl. The other children were playing on the steep slopes of the fortifications, running and shouting joyously.

"Father," said little Barbara, "look: the water lilies have gone to sleep . . . they have laid their heads on the black water. Do you think they dream when they are closed? Oh, Father, look—there is

the shipowner's daughter. . . . How pretty she is! There are pearls in her hair. . . . Is she married? How old do you have to be to get married? Father, you never answer me. Why do you look so sad?"

"I am not sad, little one," said Judocus.

"But you *are* sad, I can see it. Oh, listen! The bells are ringing. . . . Look, the moon has risen already. When the moon leaves us, where does she go?"

"Where does she go?
"Mi, do!
"Where does she go?"

sang all the bells.

"Father, put me down on the grass. I want to sit for a while. . . . Are you tired of being with me? Go and talk to Elooi and Joris Helle—they're waiting for you over there. I will watch the water and the birds and the people going by. . . . I will make myself a little wreath of daisies. . . . No, I'm not cold."

Judocus went to find his friends, who were strolling in the meadow, smoking their pipes. Little Barbara was left alone. Presently she saw a man coming toward her, followed by a band of children. He was dressed in yellow, his face was tanned, and he had a nose like Punch's. He was one of those traveling entertainers who make music with their hands and feet. He was playing a bugle, meanwhile shaking his copper hat and making the little bells on it ring. With one elbow and his heels, he worked the big drum and the cymbals which were fastened to his back.

The children had made a circle around him. "Don't stand in front of Barbara," called a big girl, "she won't be able to see. Go on, get out of the way!" Soon all had taken places and stood still. The musician had begun to play in earnest. What a strange being he was! His worn yellow costume was smocked at the shoulders, and bright little bits of looking glass were sewn onto it here and there. Barbara had never seen such a hat—a copper hat covered with bells, and pointed like a loaf of sugar. The man puffed out his cheeks and blew into his bugle. Bong! bong! he stamped on the grass, the cymbals clashed gaily behind his back, and a little doll pirouetted on top of them, swirling out her pink tarlatan skirt.

When he had finished playing, he asked for pennies. Almost all the children had some to give him. Then they went off, because it was growing dark. The musician sat down at the water's edge.

"Aren't you going too?" he asked Barbara.

"I cannot walk," she said.

"Oh, you poor child!"

"You play so well, Sir! I have no pennies, and my father is at the other end of the meadow. But here are my sleeve buttons. Take them. I think they cost a great deal. With them, you can buy plenty of bread and even some roast turkey." She had taken off her gold sleeve buttons and held them out to him.

"Keep your jewels, little girl," said the man. "A blessing on you, and your parents too. It's *I* who am going to give *you* something, because I am a wizard. Listen to what I am going to give you: one night in the year—whatever night you choose—you are going to be able to get up and go wherever you want to and

even run like other children. Tell me now, what
night will you choose? St. John's Eve, so you can
dance round the bonfires. Christmas Eve, so you can
walk to church? Or St. Nicholas' Eve, so you can go
to the shops on your own two legs? Choose.''

Barbara had turned pale. She thought a moment.

"It was skating that I liked best," she said at last, and tears ran down her cheeks.

"And what night of the year would you choose for skating? Come now, make up your mind."

"Well," said the little girl, wiping her eyes, "I choose St. Sylvain's Eve, because it always freezes hard and there's the ice carnival. And I'll be able to skate! Can it be true? And won't I die before the day comes? Holy Virgin Mary, protect me!"

"You mustn't tell a single soul!" said the strange little man. "Not anyone, do you understand? St. Sylvain's Eve . . . —and don't forget! Whatever happens that night, don't be surprised. Good-bye."

He had unfastened the strings of his cymbals. He walked away. Every now and then he gave a little skip, and all the bells on his copper hat tinkled.

"What can have set you dreaming so, my little girl," said Judocus as he carried little Barbara home.

The sky was full of stars. It seemed to Barbara as if they were already sparkling as brightly as they do on a clear, freezing night. Gently rocked by her father's footsteps, she began reckoning the months between now and winter, counting softly to herself.

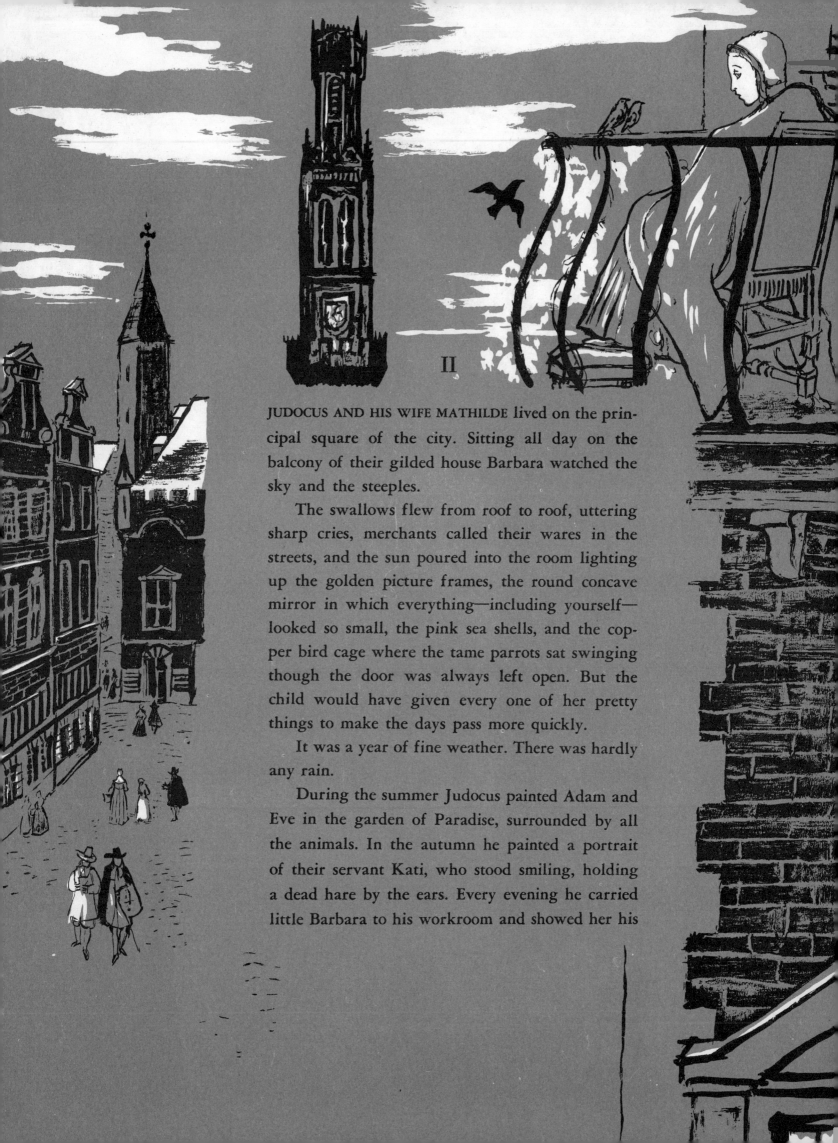

II

JUDOCUS AND HIS WIFE MATHILDE lived on the principal square of the city. Sitting all day on the balcony of their gilded house Barbara watched the sky and the steeples.

The swallows flew from roof to roof, uttering sharp cries, merchants called their wares in the streets, and the sun poured into the room lighting up the golden picture frames, the round concave mirror in which everything—including yourself—looked so small, the pink sea shells, and the copper bird cage where the tame parrots sat swinging though the door was always left open. But the child would have given every one of her pretty things to make the days pass more quickly.

It was a year of fine weather. There was hardly any rain.

During the summer Judocus painted Adam and Eve in the garden of Paradise, surrounded by all the animals. In the autumn he painted a portrait of their servant Kati, who stood smiling, holding a dead hare by the ears. Every evening he carried little Barbara to his workroom and showed her his

work. She looked at it, pressing her cheek against her father's and solemnly gave her opinion.

The harvest procession had gone by, and then the procession of Our Lady of the Sands. They had seen the charger Bayard cross the square carrying the Four Sons of Aymon, and then the Virgin Mary herself, who had come by sea in a wooden ship to wipe out all the sins of mankind.

"Peace on earth and joy in heaven," sang the little children, carrying candles through the streets.

In November it was too cold to stay by the window. A fire was lighted in Barbara's own room. To amuse her, her parents bought her a little bird from a foreign country, who ate nothing but honey. But soon it died. She cried and would not have another.

One morning when she woke she saw the roofs all furred with snow. The sky was as shining as mother-of-pearl and every sound seemed to come from the end of the world.

In December it rained. Then the ground froze again, and once more snow fell. Sitting in a corner of her father's workroom, Barbara listened to his friends talking—poets and painters, and sailors who had seen the Southern Cross on the other side of the earth. When Christmas had passed, and New Year's, and St. Sylvain's Eve was not far off, she

felt as calm as the stars in the night sky. She resigned herself. "How could I have believed all that?" she thought. "Poor Barbara! You will remain as you are, with your paralyzed legs, and neither God nor the Devil can change it!"

St. Ignatius's Day had passed, and the Feast of the Purification, and Ash Wednesday. Now only a thin veil of snow lay over the city, but the frost was hard enough to crack stones. It was almost impossible to keep the house warm. Barbara heard that there was skating on all the canals and even on the river. At last it was St. Sylvain's Eve:

"Mother," said Barbara, "aren't you and father going skating this evening as you used to when you were young? There is the Ice Festival tonight."

"We would rather stay with you, Barbara dear."

"Mother, help me put on my sable coat. Thank you. Open the window. Carry me, please; I want to see the children, yes I want to sit on the window sill . . . that's right . . . thank you, Mother."

Presently she saw some boys pass, returning home through the city with their skates in their hands.

"There's a black frost, little Barbara," they said. "This evening we shall go back to the river for the great festival! There is to be a man who cooks waffles while he dances on a tightrope and then throws them to the skaters!"

"Have a good time!" Barbara cried. Her fresh voice trembled and broke in the winter wind.

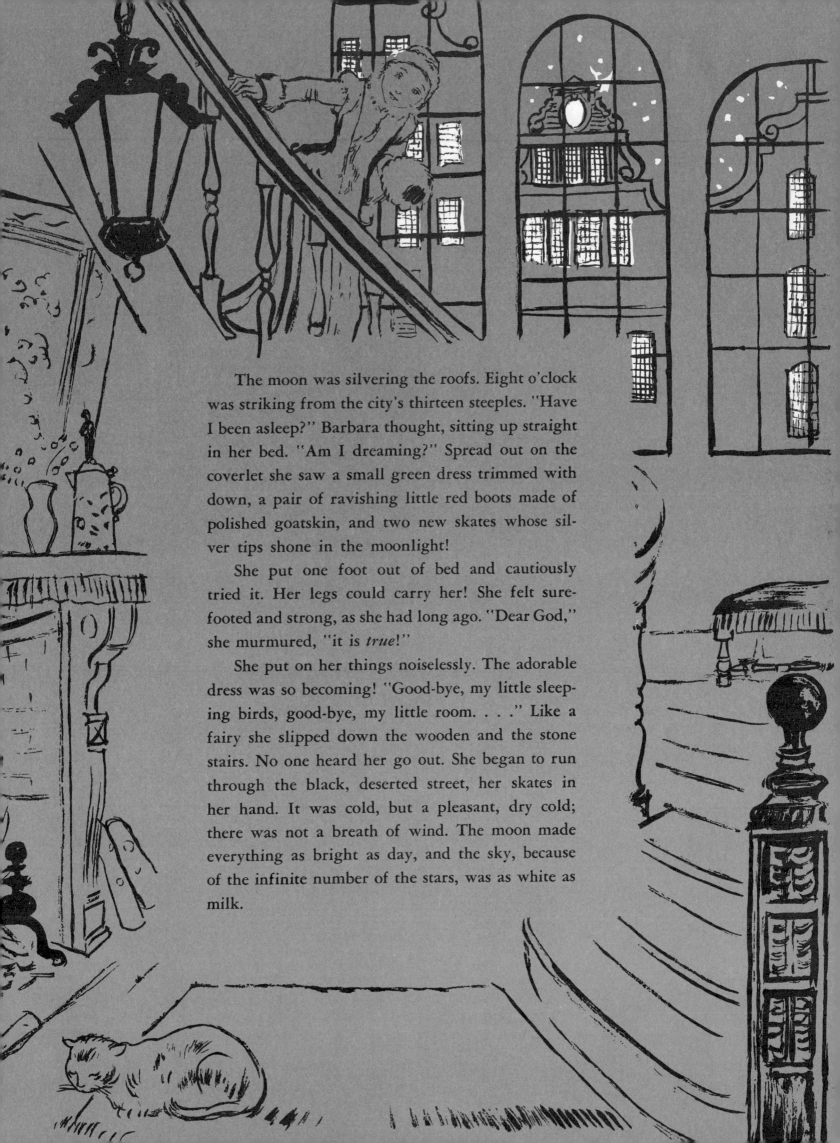

The moon was silvering the roofs. Eight o'clock was striking from the city's thirteen steeples. "Have I been asleep?" Barbara thought, sitting up straight in her bed. "Am I dreaming?" Spread out on the coverlet she saw a small green dress trimmed with down, a pair of ravishing little red boots made of polished goatskin, and two new skates whose silver tips shone in the moonlight!

She put one foot out of bed and cautiously tried it. Her legs could carry her! She felt sure-footed and strong, as she had long ago. "Dear God," she murmured, "it is *true*!"

She put on her things noiselessly. The adorable dress was so becoming! "Good-bye, my little sleeping birds, good-bye, my little room. . . ." Like a fairy she slipped down the wooden and the stone stairs. No one heard her go out. She began to run through the black, deserted street, her skates in her hand. It was cold, but a pleasant, dry cold; there was not a breath of wind. The moon made everything as bright as day, and the sky, because of the infinite number of the stars, was as white as milk.

Nowadays winters are not so icy, and the earth will doubtless turn for a long time before those old-fashioned seasons come back when the canals stayed frozen for ten weeks between two rows of reeds glittering with frost, when peasants came up the rivers all the way to the cities in red and green sleighs for the evening festivals in February.

"What thick ice!" Barbara thought when she came to the edge of the canal "—hard as rock, and so black and bright."

Where were the fish and the waterlilies and the fat frogs of summer?

That day almost all the townspeople had gathered on the ice, where the lamps were reflected

with many-colored halos. From the shining center of the festival came a confused noise, and all around was the sound of sleighbells and the squeaking of runners on the packed snow. From time to time young people in masks and costumes came close to the bank, calling out joyously.

Barbara fastened on her skates. She was trembling with impatience, and also with fear. Would she be able to stay on her feet, like all those healthy little girls? But from her very first strokes—oh, happiness!—she felt herself being effortlessly carried over the smooth black ice. Soon she was surrounded by a troop of children in costumes. "Where are you from," they cried, "little girl in green? What a lovely green coat trimmed with down! How well you skate!"

Rosy with the cold, she smiled and glided on without answering, pressing her lips against her feather muff.

"Why, it's you, Barbara!" a little girl exclaimed. "Have you gotten well? Come and skate with us!"

She followed them, intoxicated with joy. She raced, outstripped them all, then came back to meet them after making a graceful turn on one foot. It was just as it used to be! . . . It was happiness come again! She must not think of tomorrow, or of yesterday, she must only glide, glide, faster and still faster, over the black crystal, drinking in the joy of her speed, drinking in the cold. . . .

The night was dark blue. Far away, the towers of the city were wrapped in a vague brightness. Barbara heard it strike ten. She saw that she had left the other children behind; she had passed the last skaters and, far from the lights and the noise, she was gliding away down the great frozen river.

Faster, still faster! Barbara had never skated so fast—never. . . . She flew like a wild bird! The city had disappeared. There was nothing but flat fields, dark and deserted. And soon she could no longer see the banks at all. She was alone between the ice and the starry sky!

At the bend of the river, where it divided before flowing on still farther to throw itself into sea, she came upon a black shape that blocked the sky and hid part of the stars. It was a ship caught in the ice. Yes, it was a ship with three masts, an old-fashioned ship with a mermaid for a figurehead. The sails hung half out of their covers, stiff with frost. On

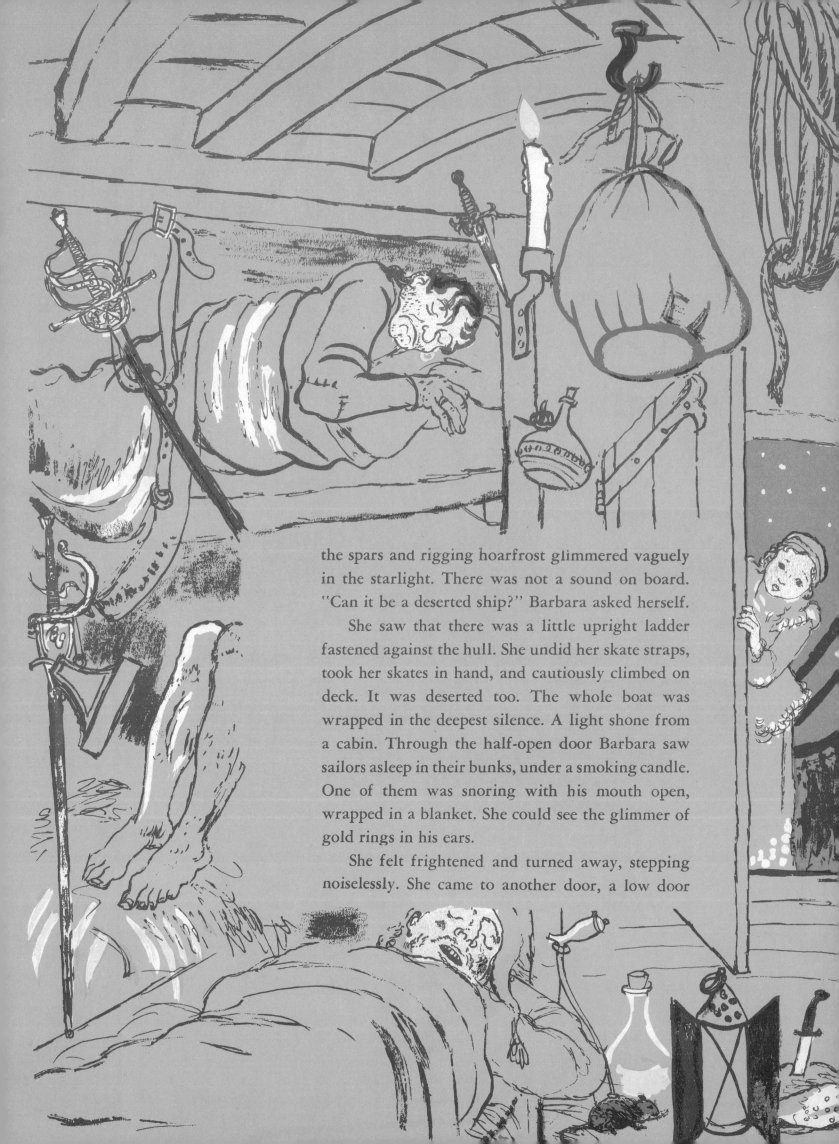

the spars and rigging hoarfrost glimmered vaguely in the starlight. There was not a sound on board. "Can it be a deserted ship?" Barbara asked herself.

She saw that there was a little upright ladder fastened against the hull. She undid her skate straps, took her skates in hand, and cautiously climbed on deck. It was deserted too. The whole boat was wrapped in the deepest silence. A light shone from a cabin. Through the half-open door Barbara saw sailors asleep in their bunks, under a smoking candle. One of them was snoring with his mouth open, wrapped in a blanket. She could see the glimmer of gold rings in his ears.

She felt frightened and turned away, stepping noiselessly. She came to another door, a low door

of carved mahogany, decorated with a pair of dolphins. She knocked. No one answered. She turned the handle. The door opened silently and Barbara smelled the mingled odors of a good meal. There were three steps to go down. . . . She found herself in a small room with walls of rare wood, lighted by a lamp that hung from the ceiling. On a narrow bed beside a table loaded with dishes and flagons a captain had fallen asleep. He was a gray-haired man, dressed in a suit of faded velvet. He had taken off his boots and lay sleeping among a disorderly array of cushions, his legs crossed, his hands under his head.

Barbara looked the cabin all over carefully, from its curved ceiling down. It was warm and inviting. Finally, as the captain kept on sleeping,

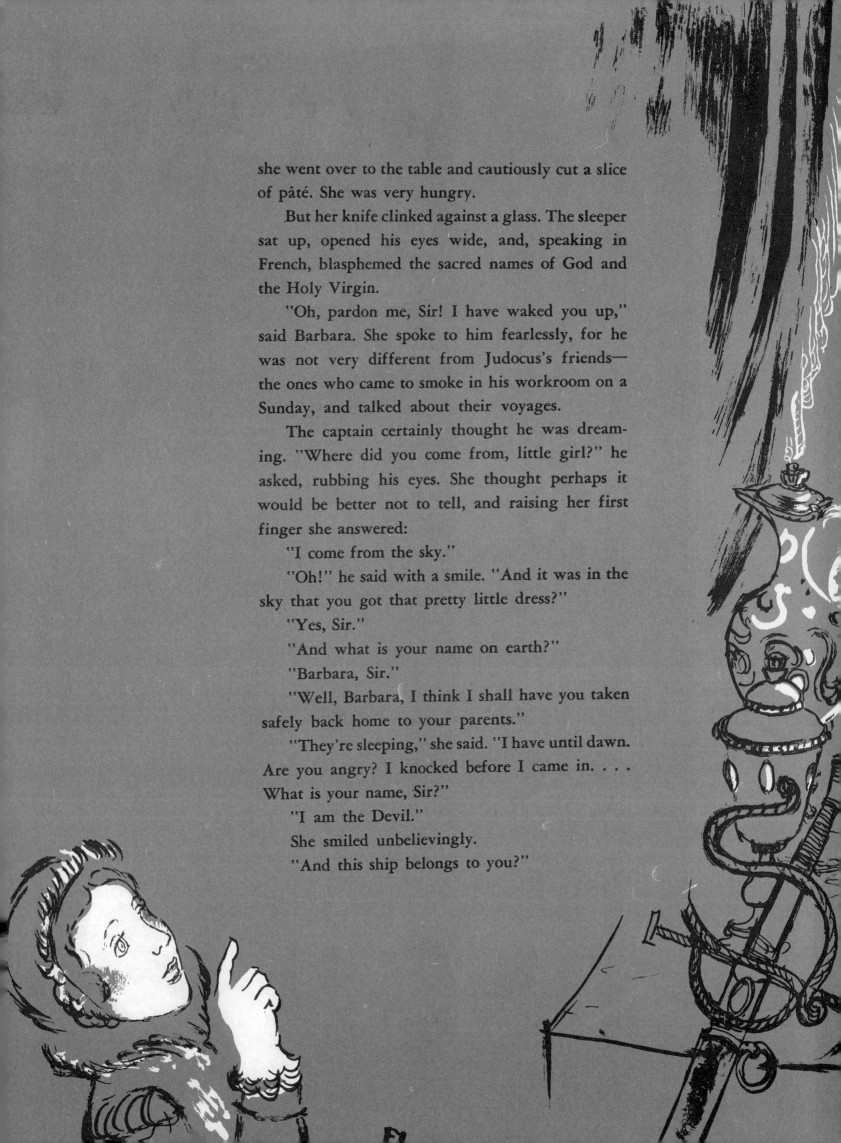

she went over to the table and cautiously cut a slice of pâté. She was very hungry.

But her knife clinked against a glass. The sleeper sat up, opened his eyes wide, and, speaking in French, blasphemed the sacred names of God and the Holy Virgin.

"Oh, pardon me, Sir! I have waked you up," said Barbara. She spoke to him fearlessly, for he was not very different from Judocus's friends—the ones who came to smoke in his workroom on a Sunday, and talked about their voyages.

The captain certainly thought he was dreaming. "Where did you come from, little girl?" he asked, rubbing his eyes. She thought perhaps it would be better not to tell, and raising her first finger she answered:

"I come from the sky."

"Oh!" he said with a smile. "And it was in the sky that you got that pretty little dress?"

"Yes, Sir."

"And what is your name on earth?"

"Barbara, Sir."

"Well, Barbara, I think I shall have you taken safely back home to your parents."

"They're sleeping," she said. "I have until dawn. Are you angry? I knocked before I came in. . . . What is your name, Sir?"

"I am the Devil."

She smiled unbelievingly.

"And this ship belongs to you?"

"Yes, it is mine. And everything in it too."

"May I see your ship?"

"Oh no! That's against the rules, child."

He was smiling now too. He leaned across the table. His pale, strange face had something shocking in it. But Barbara felt that the captain was her friend. "Sir," she said, "I will tell you everything, if you will swear by Our Lord that you will not repeat it to anyone in the world?"

The man thought for a moment. "All right, little girl," he said. "I'll promise you that."

"Good! Then it shall be a secret between us two. Listen! This is the truth: All year long I am paralyzed. All year long, and all my life long, I think. But because of a charm, I can come and go on one night of each year—a single night, tonight, St. Sylvain's Eve. So you really ought to show me all the fine things you have to show, oughtn't you? And I will pray for your soul every day, as long as God gives me life."

"Oh," said the captain, "that will take many prayers! But you can only walk on one night in the year? And what do you do the rest of the year, my poor child?"

"I watch my father work. I watch the sky and the steeples. I know how to make lace with three hundred bobbins! And I think. . . ."

"And no one knows that you have come all the way here?"

"No, Sir."

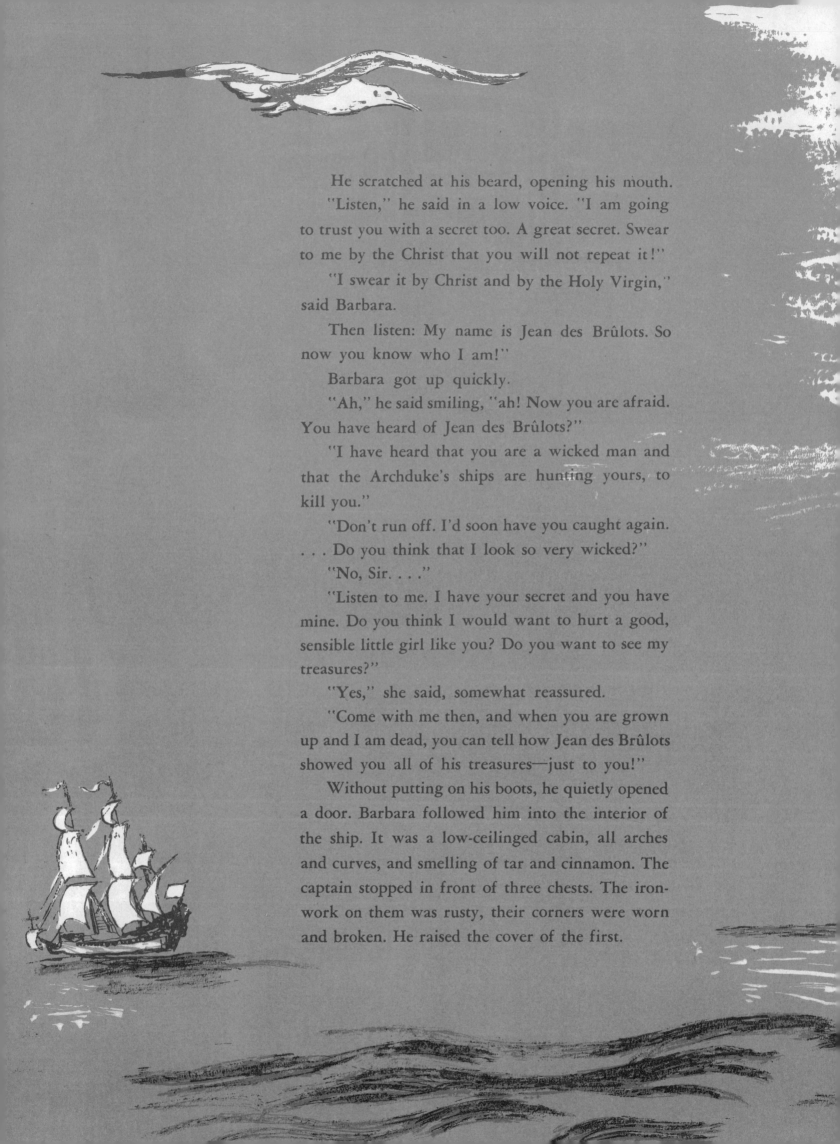

He scratched at his beard, opening his mouth.

"Listen," he said in a low voice. "I am going to trust you with a secret too. A great secret. Swear to me by the Christ that you will not repeat it!"

"I swear it by Christ and by the Holy Virgin," said Barbara.

Then listen: My name is Jean des Brûlots. So now you know who I am!"

Barbara got up quickly.

"Ah," he said smiling, "ah! Now you are afraid. You have heard of Jean des Brûlots?"

"I have heard that you are a wicked man and that the Archduke's ships are hunting yours, to kill you."

"Don't run off. I'd soon have you caught again. . . . Do you think that I look so very wicked?"

"No, Sir. . . ."

"Listen to me. I have your secret and you have mine. Do you think I would want to hurt a good, sensible little girl like you? Do you want to see my treasures?"

"Yes," she said, somewhat reassured.

"Come with me then, and when you are grown up and I am dead, you can tell how Jean des Brûlots showed you all of his treasures—just to you!"

Without putting on his boots, he quietly opened a door. Barbara followed him into the interior of the ship. It was a low-ceilinged cabin, all arches and curves, and smelling of tar and cinnamon. The captain stopped in front of three chests. The iron-work on them was rusty, their corners were worn and broken. He raised the cover of the first.

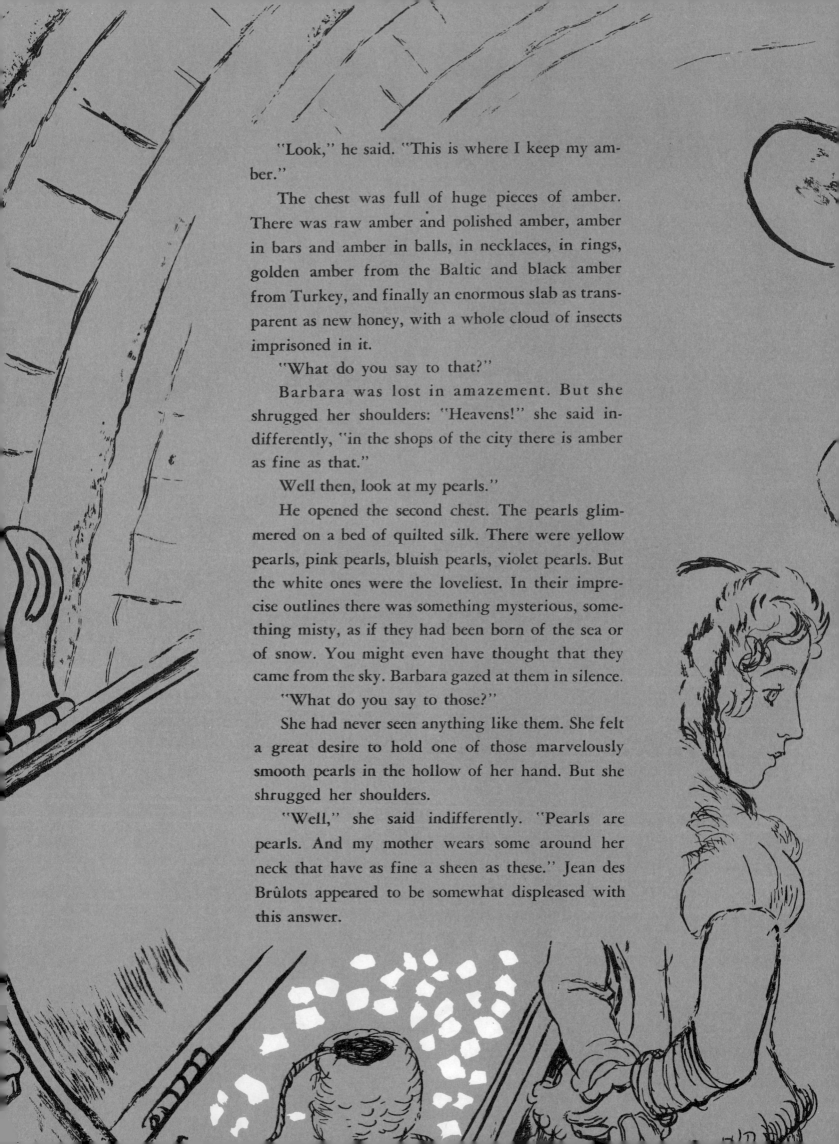

"Look," he said. "This is where I keep my amber."

The chest was full of huge pieces of amber. There was raw amber and polished amber, amber in bars and amber in balls, in necklaces, in rings, golden amber from the Baltic and black amber from Turkey, and finally an enormous slab as transparent as new honey, with a whole cloud of insects imprisoned in it.

"What do you say to that?"

Barbara was lost in amazement. But she shrugged her shoulders: "Heavens!" she said indifferently, "in the shops of the city there is amber as fine as that."

Well then, look at my pearls."

He opened the second chest. The pearls glimmered on a bed of quilted silk. There were yellow pearls, pink pearls, bluish pearls, violet pearls. But the white ones were the loveliest. In their imprecise outlines there was something mysterious, something misty, as if they had been born of the sea or of snow. You might even have thought that they came from the sky. Barbara gazed at them in silence.

"What do you say to those?"

She had never seen anything like them. She felt a great desire to hold one of those marvelously smooth pearls in the hollow of her hand. But she shrugged her shoulders.

"Well," she said indifferently. "Pearls are pearls. And my mother wears some around her neck that have as fine a sheen as these." Jean des Brûlots appeared to be somewhat displeased with this answer.

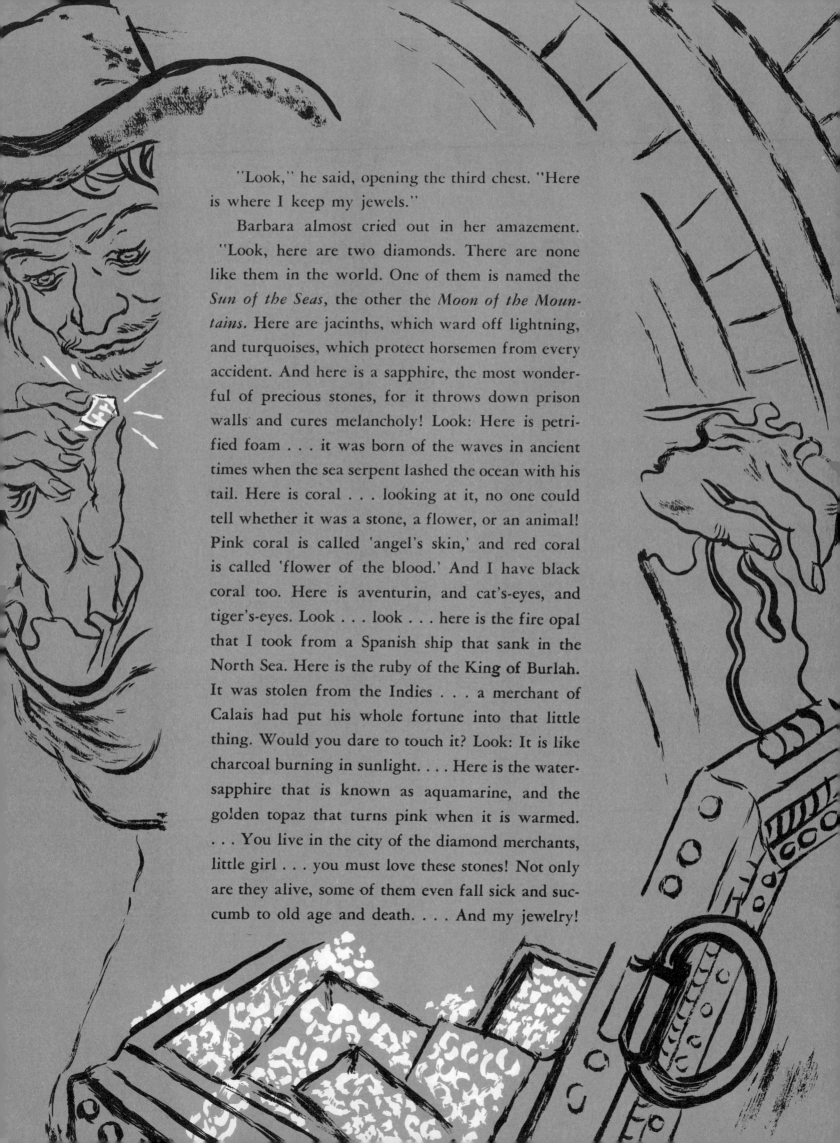

"Look," he said, opening the third chest. "Here is where I keep my jewels."

Barbara almost cried out in her amazement. "Look, here are two diamonds. There are none like them in the world. One of them is named the *Sun of the Seas*, the other the *Moon of the Mountains*. Here are jacinths, which ward off lightning, and turquoises, which protect horsemen from every accident. And here is a sapphire, the most wonderful of precious stones, for it throws down prison walls and cures melancholy! Look: Here is petrified foam . . . it was born of the waves in ancient times when the sea serpent lashed the ocean with his tail. Here is coral . . . looking at it, no one could tell whether it was a stone, a flower, or an animal! Pink coral is called 'angel's skin,' and red coral is called 'flower of the blood.' And I have black coral too. Here is aventurin, and cat's-eyes, and tiger's-eyes. Look . . . look . . . here is the fire opal that I took from a Spanish ship that sank in the North Sea. Here is the ruby of the King of Burlah. It was stolen from the Indies . . . a merchant of Calais had put his whole fortune into that little thing. Would you dare to touch it? Look: It is like charcoal burning in sunlight. . . . Here is the water-sapphire that is known as aquamarine, and the golden topaz that turns pink when it is warmed. . . . You live in the city of the diamond merchants, little girl . . . you must love these stones! Not only are they alive, some of them even fall sick and succumb to old age and death. . . . And my jewelry!

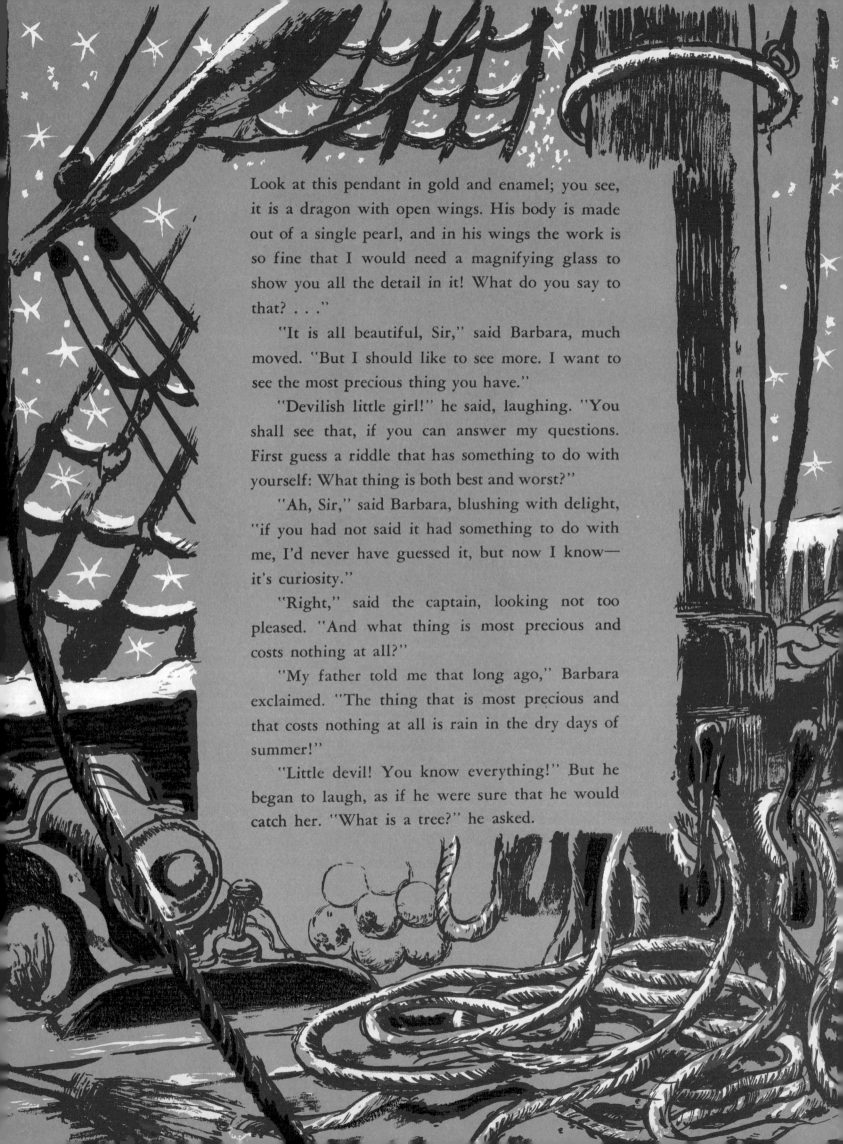

Look at this pendant in gold and enamel; you see, it is a dragon with open wings. His body is made out of a single pearl, and in his wings the work is so fine that I would need a magnifying glass to show you all the detail in it! What do you say to that? . . ."

"It is all beautiful, Sir," said Barbara, much moved. "But I should like to see more. I want to see the most precious thing you have."

"Devilish little girl!" he said, laughing. "You shall see that, if you can answer my questions. First guess a riddle that has something to do with yourself: What thing is both best and worst?"

"Ah, Sir," said Barbara, blushing with delight, "if you had not said it had something to do with me, I'd never have guessed it, but now I know— it's curiosity."

"Right," said the captain, looking not too pleased. "And what thing is most precious and costs nothing at all?"

"My father told me that long ago," Barbara exclaimed. "The thing that is most precious and that costs nothing at all is rain in the dry days of summer!"

"Little devil! You know everything!" But he began to laugh, as if he were sure that he would catch her. "What is a tree?" he asked.

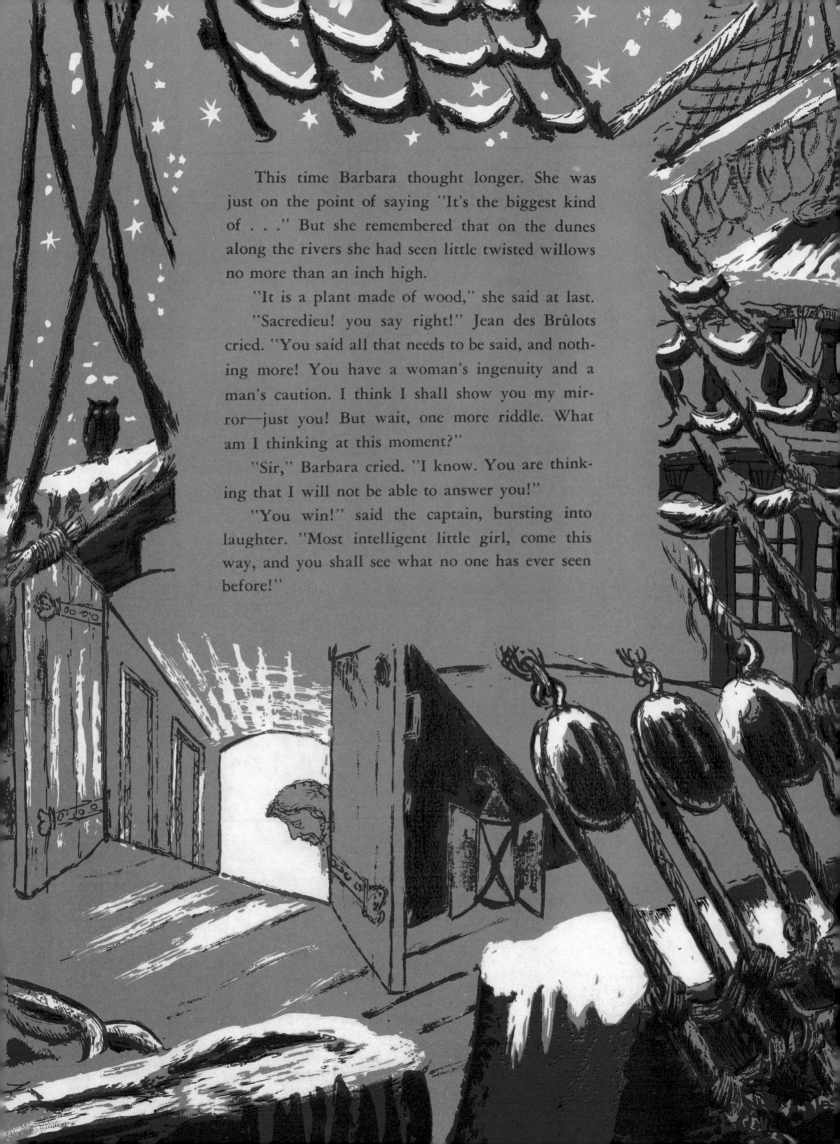

This time Barbara thought longer. She was just on the point of saying "It's the biggest kind of . . ." But she remembered that on the dunes along the rivers she had seen little twisted willows no more than an inch high.

"It is a plant made of wood," she said at last.

"Sacredieu! you say right!" Jean des Brûlots cried. "You said all that needs to be said, and nothing more! You have a woman's ingenuity and a man's caution. I think I shall show you my mirror—just you! But wait, one more riddle. What am I thinking at this moment?"

"Sir," Barbara cried, "I know. You are thinking that I will not be able to answer you!"

"You win!" said the captain, bursting into laughter. "Most intelligent little girl, come this way, and you shall see what no one has ever seen before!"

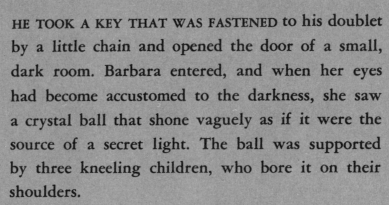

III

HE TOOK A KEY THAT WAS FASTENED to his doublet by a little chain and opened the door of a small, dark room. Barbara entered, and when her eyes had become accustomed to the darkness, she saw a crystal ball that shone vaguely as if it were the source of a secret light. The ball was supported by three kneeling children, who bore it on their shoulders.

"Shhh!" said Jean des Brulots, "they are asleep. . ."

"Oh!" said Barbara softly. "Who are they? They are so beautiful!"

"The little girl who is so sound asleep is Memory. The least thing will waken her. . . . I let her sleep as long as possible—she is often tired of bearing the mirror of the world!"

"And the little boy with his eyes half open—who is he?"

"He is Dream."

"And the beautiful little girl?"

"She is Imagination."

"Are they going to stay asleep?"

"No. You shall wake them by breathing on them."

"Oh, the poor little things! I don't want to frighten them. . . ."

"Don't worry—they are not easily frightened! Wake Memory first. And mind you look carefully at what she shows you."

As soon as she felt Barbara's breath on her hair the child whom Jean des Brûlots called Memory opened her eyes and fixed them on the mirror

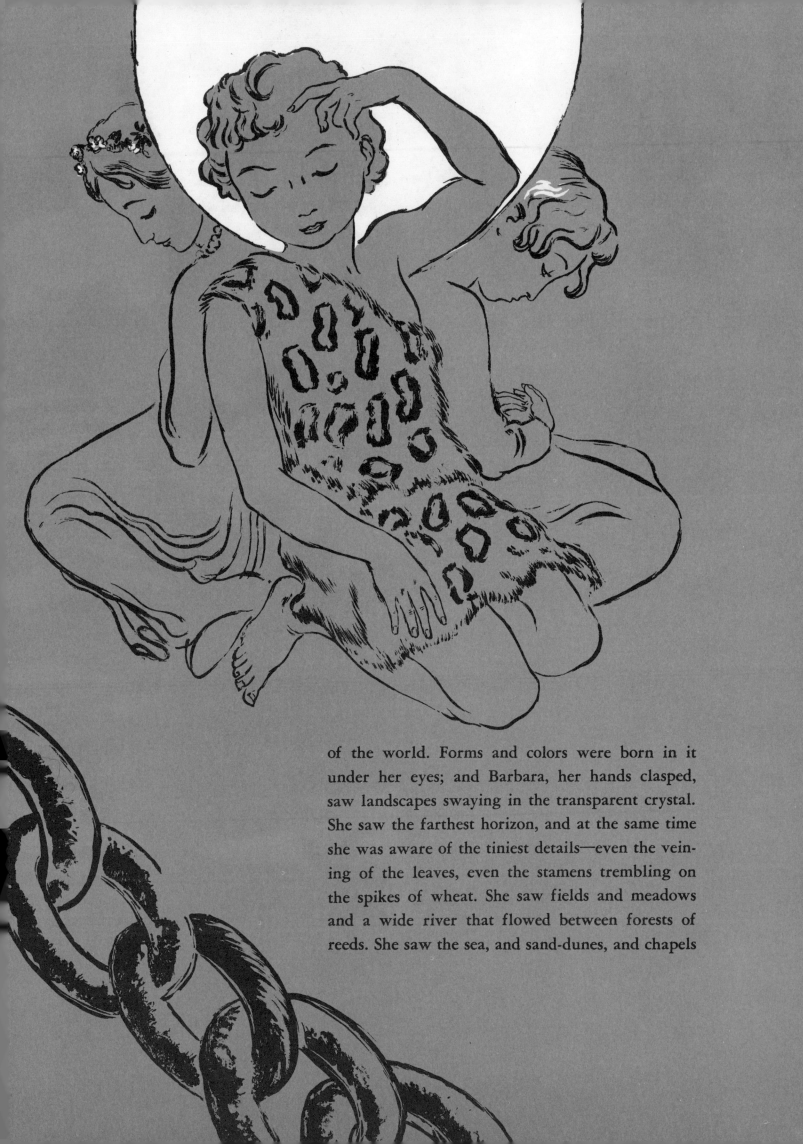

of the world. Forms and colors were born in it under her eyes; and Barbara, her hands clasped, saw landscapes swaying in the transparent crystal. She saw the farthest horizon, and at the same time she was aware of the tiniest details—even the veining of the leaves, even the stamens trembling on the spikes of wheat. She saw fields and meadows and a wide river that flowed between forests of reeds. She saw the sea, and sand-dunes, and chapels

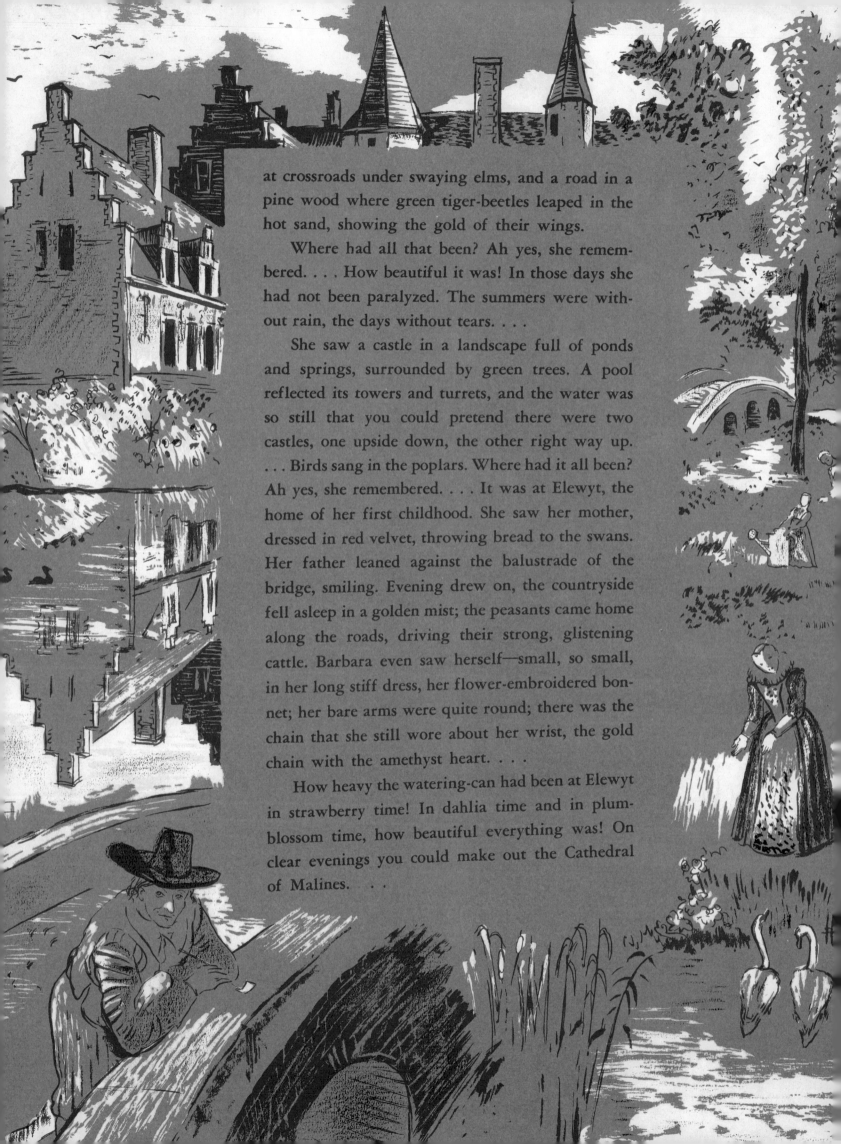

at crossroads under swaying elms, and a road in a pine wood where green tiger-beetles leaped in the hot sand, showing the gold of their wings.

Where had all that been? Ah yes, she remembered. . . . How beautiful it was! In those days she had not been paralyzed. The summers were without rain, the days without tears. . . .

She saw a castle in a landscape full of ponds and springs, surrounded by green trees. A pool reflected its towers and turrets, and the water was so still that you could pretend there were two castles, one upside down, the other right way up. . . . Birds sang in the poplars. Where had it all been? Ah yes, she remembered. . . . It was at Elewyt, the home of her first childhood. She saw her mother, dressed in red velvet, throwing bread to the swans. Her father leaned against the balustrade of the bridge, smiling. Evening drew on, the countryside fell asleep in a golden mist; the peasants came home along the roads, driving their strong, glistening cattle. Barbara even saw herself—small, so small, in her long stiff dress, her flower-embroidered bonnet; her bare arms were quite round; there was the chain that she still wore about her wrist, the gold chain with the amethyst heart. . . .

How heavy the watering-can had been at Elewyt in strawberry time! In dahlia time and in plum-blossom time, how beautiful everything was! On clear evenings you could make out the Cathedral of Malines. . . .

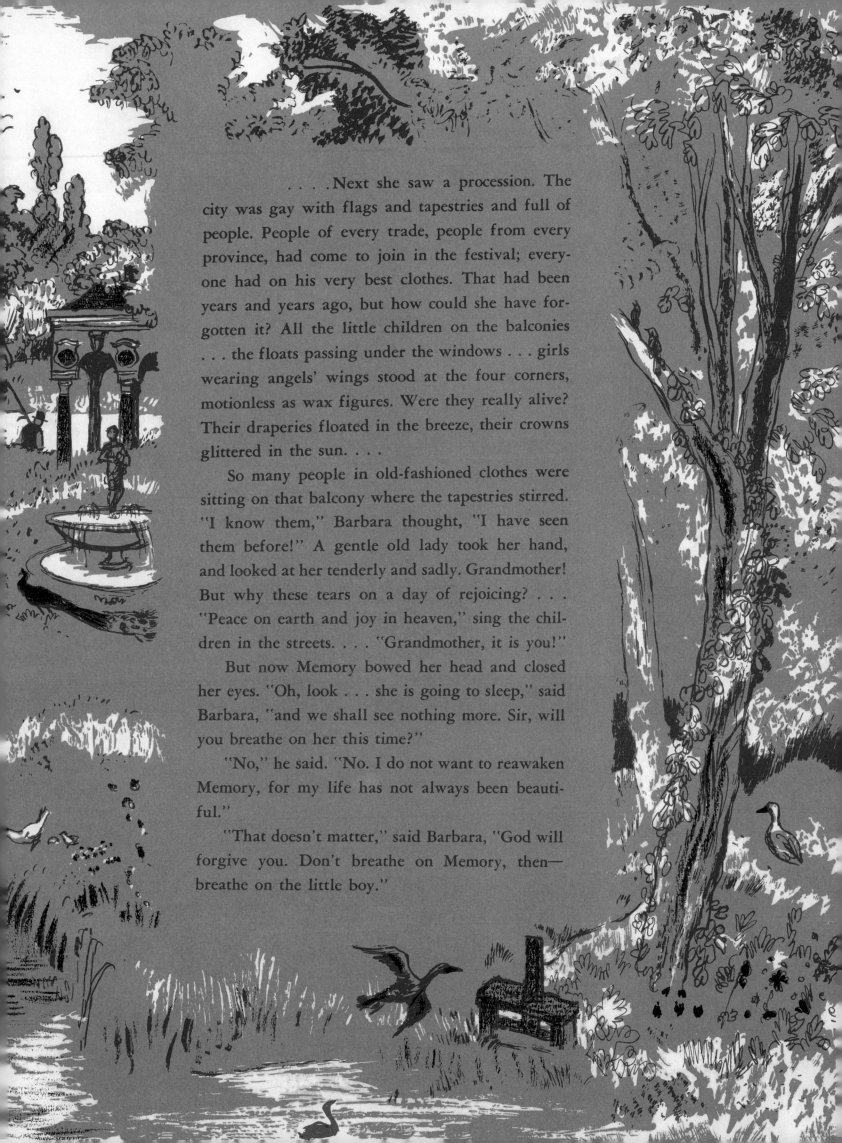

. . . . Next she saw a procession. The city was gay with flags and tapestries and full of people. People of every trade, people from every province, had come to join in the festival; everyone had on his very best clothes. That had been years and years ago, but how could she have forgotten it? All the little children on the balconies . . . the floats passing under the windows . . . girls wearing angels' wings stood at the four corners, motionless as wax figures. Were they really alive? Their draperies floated in the breeze, their crowns glittered in the sun. . . .

So many people in old-fashioned clothes were sitting on that balcony where the tapestries stirred. "I know them," Barbara thought, "I have seen them before!" A gentle old lady took her hand, and looked at her tenderly and sadly. Grandmother! But why these tears on a day of rejoicing? . . . "Peace on earth and joy in heaven," sing the children in the streets. . . . "Grandmother, it is you!"

But now Memory bowed her head and closed her eyes. "Oh, look . . . she is going to sleep," said Barbara, "and we shall see nothing more. Sir, will you breathe on her this time?"

"No," he said. "No. I do not want to reawaken Memory, for my life has not always been beautiful."

"That doesn't matter," said Barbara, "God will forgive you. Don't breathe on Memory, then—breathe on the little boy."

"No," said Jean des Brûlots, "no. . . . Do it yourself."

Barbara breathed on the hair of Dream; the boy stretched gently, pushing back his garment of panther skin. He did not quite wake up, but he rested his cheek against the crystal ball. And what Barbara saw then, she had never seen before—no, never! Of that she was perfectly sure. Perhaps long ago someone had read her a story and in the story there had been this lovely landscape. . . . Was it the New World? She saw a delicious valley, a perfect paradise. On the horizon, blue mountains covered with forests. Through the depths of the valley flowed a river, moving on toward the plain under bridges of tangled lianas. A canoe glided over the water, and copper-skinned men crowned with feathers shot arrows at the birds along the banks.

The landscape in the crystal ball changed. Now there were immense solitudes over which herds of horses passed. The proud beasts fled at the slightest sound, tossing their long manes, racing with each other, then suddenly stopped short, necks stretched out, ears up, nostrils open, their innocent and fiery eyes questioning every corner of the horizon.

The sea! Barbara saw a ship at sea. She followed it close, as if she had been able to fly. . . . It was a square three-master, pitching violently; every time it came down the bowsprit went under, send-

ing up a bouquet of foam. Everyone on board was
about some task; everywhere were signs of dis-
order, of work left undone for lack of strength to
do it. The deck was water-logged. There were only
a few sails left. She soon understood the reason:
a storm had passed over the ship and all the sailors
were busy repairing the damage the hurricane had
done. It was then that she saw a black cloud come
up and swoop down on the ship and envelop it—
it was thousands of birds! They completely covered the deck and found their way inside the ship
through every porthole.

"Oh, the poor things," she said, "they are dead
tired!" And indeed the birds seemed to have reached
the end of their strength.

Like the sailors, they must have been swept from their course for hours by the cyclone, and the ship was the only place in all that vast sea where they could find refuge. Barbara knew them well —among them were all the land birds you could ever dream of: thrushes, turtle-doves, orioles, warblers, swallows, but above all canaries and bluebirds. The sailors picked the most exhausted ones up from the deck, and they let themselves be handled without showing any signs of fear. All the rigging, everything that could serve as a perch, was covered with birds. They remained for a long time. The men sat down wherever the people of the air left them room; and you could see that they were thinking of spring in their own lands.

"Sir," said Barbara, deeply touched, "last year a captain told my father the story of these birds, I was sitting in his workroom . . . listening . . . I. . . ."

"Look, child, there is something else coming. . . ."

"Oh!" said Barbara, "it is the poet who sleeps in the porcelain pavilion! I don't know what country it's in. . . . I don't remember who told me about it. . . . Look. There are black pines on the rocks, and the crests of the waves are like curls; how lovely it is! You would say it was a picture painted on silk. . . ."

There were peasants with yellow hats crossing

a ford; before they went into the water they pulled up their long robes.

In a pine wood an emperor on horseback met a goddess who hid her face behind a golden fan. And, right at the edge of the sea, on a rock on which the waves broke, a boy was flying a parchment kite as round and white as the moon. . . .

But Dream let his head fall on his shoulder, and there were no more pictures in the crystal ball.

"Sir Captain," Barbara exclaimed, "will you let me breathe on Imagination too?"

"Certainly."

"Heavens," she said, clasping her hands, "perhaps it would be better to let her sleep?"

But she breathed on her.

Then Imagination stretched out her thin graceful arms, she half opened her eyes and laid her hand on the crystal ball, her gaze would not rest on anything that was around her, but seemed to fix itself on something far beyond.

And the air began to vibrate and swell with a delicious sound. It was the voice of the wind in a sail, the murmur of the breeze over islands where no one has ever gone! In the dark night there appeared a distant star, shining as if lighted for a festival to which none might find the way. The stars danced in the infinite sky, strewing it with powdered gold.

And then it was dawn. Descending by paths of light Barbara saw ravishing children who seemed to know no more of laughter than they knew of tears. Their feet just touched the clouds, their hands were stretched toward her, their eyes sought hers, tenderly, comprehendingly, and seemed to say:

"Is it you? . . . We shall meet again in the gardens of Heaven."

"Don't cry, child," said Jean des Brûlots, who had taken Barbara back to his cabin. "Don't cry. All that you have seen, you will see again next year. And now, good-bye. . . . It will soon be dawn. Put on your skates and hurry back. Try to be happy all through the year, remembering St. Sylvain's Eve. And remember that no one in the world can see what you have seen!"

They went on deck. It was bitter cold. The
sailors had not awakened. Barbara could think of
nothing but her parents.

"O Lord Jesus," she prayed, "let me get home
before You put out the stars!"

"Don't worry, child," said Jean des Brûlots,
"the city is not far away. Skate fast. Good-bye! Until next year . . . !"

She struck out over the ice.

IV

CHRISTMAS EVE HAD BEEN CLEAR and cold, and spring came early that year. The Sunday before Easter Judocus carried his little daughter out to the slopes outside the city, so that she could see the countryside in its new dress of green.

"Father," she said, "put me down on the grass; yes do, it has been such a long time. . . . How lovely everything is! Look, there are some pink daisies. . . . When will the storks come back? Yes, sit me down on your cloak. You can take a little walk. I'll stay here. The children will come and talk to me. . . ."

Judocus went to walk by the waterside. He often turned round to look back at his Barbara, his Battie, who grew smaller and smaller as he got farther away. Sometimes he waved his hand to her.

A little girl left a round dance to come and sit down, quite breathless. She spread out her skirt like a grownup.

"Oh, Battie, it's you! Good morning! You have a new pink dress for spring? How pretty you look! Have you heard? Listen: St. Sylvain's Eve we skated on the river with a little girl who didn't come from the city; she looked exactly like you. We thought it was you and that you had gotten well! She had such a pretty velvet dress trimmed with down! She went off, and we didn't see her again. What a good time we had that night! Dear Barbara, it's a shame that you are always ill, otherwise you could play tag with us, or 'I'm the King of the Castle.' You'd like to, wouldn't you? I have to go . . . they're calling me. Good-bye!"

Barbara bent her head to hide her eyes and her lips. Her heart was filled with bitterness. Must it always be like this? Must she always be plunged back into life, and suffer, suffer, until the hour of her death?

It was exactly like last year. She saw the traveling musician in his yellow suit come toward her, followed by a band of children. Again he played his strange, lovely music. When the children had scattered after giving him their pennies, he sat down beside her and looked at her; interest and compassion in his eyes.

"Well, little girl," he asked, "you are not happy?"

"No," said Barbara, holding back her tears.

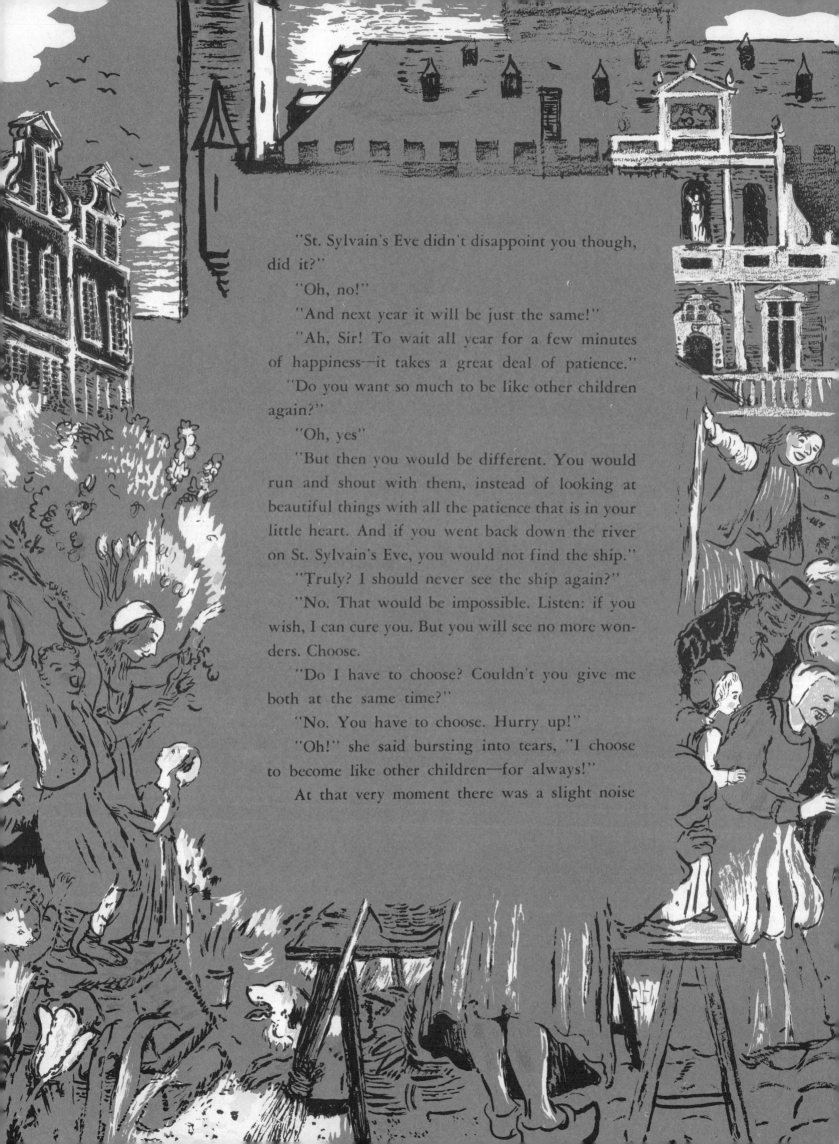

"St. Sylvain's Eve didn't disappoint you though, did it?"

"Oh, no!"

"And next year it will be just the same!"

"Ah, Sir! To wait all year for a few minutes of happiness—it takes a great deal of patience."

"Do you want so much to be like other children again?"

"Oh, yes"

"But then you would be different. You would run and shout with them, instead of looking at beautiful things with all the patience that is in your little heart. And if you went back down the river on St. Sylvain's Eve, you would not find the ship."

"Truly? I should never see the ship again?"

"No. That would be impossible. Listen: if you wish, I can cure you. But you will see no more wonders. Choose.

"Do I have to choose? Couldn't you give me both at the same time?"

"No. You have to choose. Hurry up!"

"Oh!" she said bursting into tears, "I choose to become like other children—for always!"

At that very moment there was a slight noise

in the air, the noise of a squib. The yellow man had disappeared. Barbara stood up straight and walked across the meadow to meet her father. For a week, the whole city talked about nothing but the miracle.

An old woman who kept a shop on the principal square said, raising her cane:

"I know what made Battie well; it was I who told her mother how to cure her. I told her to lay her in front of the fire every night, naked, and rub her back and legs with a chunk of bacon, and pray as hard as she could to St. Barbara. . . . And there you are!"

"I was never rubbed with bacon!" Barbara exclaimed, shrugging her shoulders. And then she laughed like mad and climbed up onto the tulip seller's stall with the other children. She picked up a cabbage leaf and put it on her head. Ah, if only you knew! It was tulip and hyacinth week, and in the market place there were all those lovely colors and it smelled so sweet that it finally made you sick. "There's mother calling me," said Barbara. "I must go home. What a day!"

Judocus and Mathilde were very happy. Now they had a beautiful little girl with agile legs, who slipped downstairs like a cat, who ran and shouted

for joy on the slopes of the fortifications with all the other children in the city Sometimes they were astonished to see how vivacious she was. "But she will still be sweet and good," they thought, "because nothing can change our hearts."

The whole year passed in pleasures. Judocus was painting a big portrait of his little Barbara, a wonderful portrait in which she was standing there in a dress that was dark and shining like a laurel leaf, with a lace collar; standing with a tulip in her hand, her cheeks all rosy, her lips parted, in the middle of a field of soft grass in which lambs were playing.

She insisted that in the background her father must paint a musician in yellow wearing a hat with bells. "Why?" Judocus asked. "Father dear," said she, "please do it—please! You saw the man who

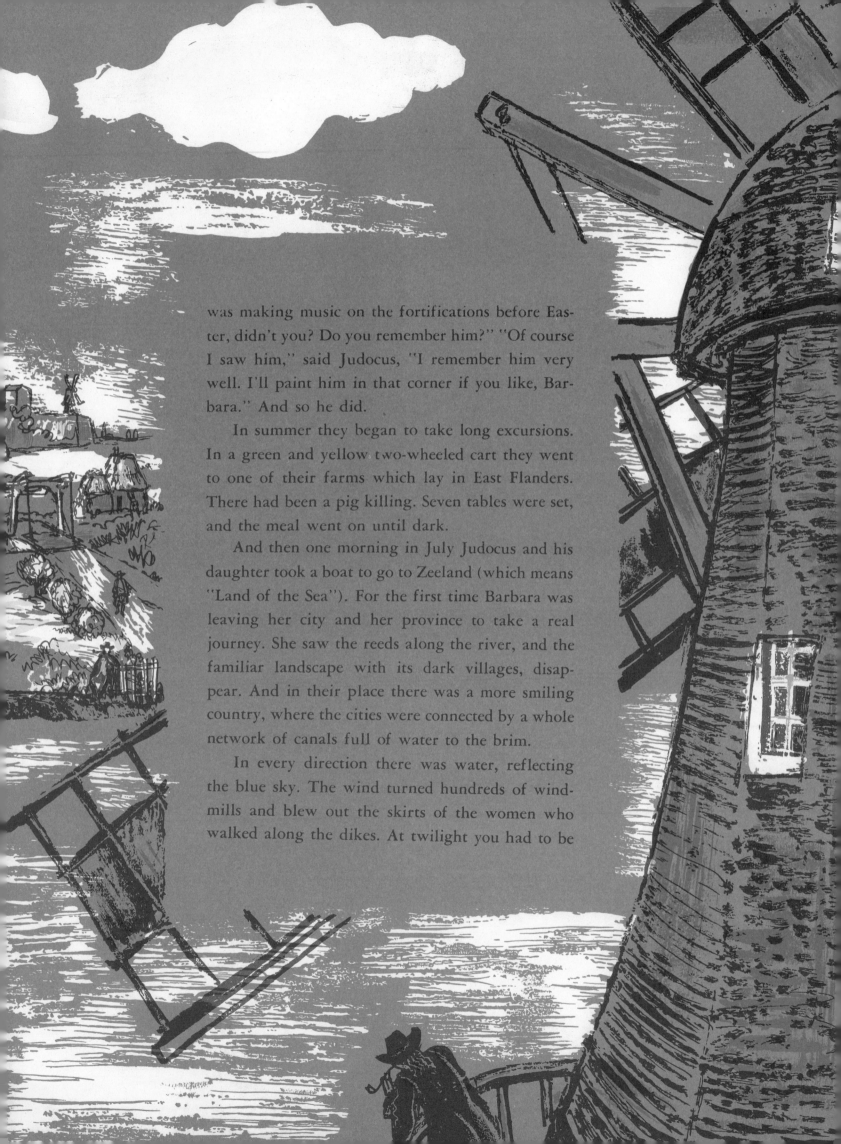

was making music on the fortifications before Easter, didn't you? Do you remember him?" "Of course I saw him," said Judocus, "I remember him very well. I'll paint him in that corner if you like, Barbara." And so he did.

In summer they began to take long excursions. In a green and yellow two-wheeled cart they went to one of their farms which lay in East Flanders. There had been a pig killing. Seven tables were set, and the meal went on until dark.

And then one morning in July Judocus and his daughter took a boat to go to Zeeland (which means "Land of the Sea"). For the first time Barbara was leaving her city and her province to take a real journey. She saw the reeds along the river, and the familiar landscape with its dark villages, disappear. And in their place there was a more smiling country, where the cities were connected by a whole network of canals full of water to the brim.

In every direction there was water, reflecting the blue sky. The wind turned hundreds of windmills and blew out the skirts of the women who walked along the dikes. At twilight you had to be

quite close to a town to see its steeples, they were so wrapped in blue haze.

"Farther on," said Judocus, pointing to the sea, "there is the Ocean, and on the other side of the Ocean there is the New World, and still farther there is Asia!"

"I know," said Barbara. She was thinking of Jean des Brûlot's ship and of the magic mirror.

In July the days had already begun to shorten again. The heavy yellow moon of summer evenings lifted itself laboriously over the meadows and the fortifications; and very little children thought they could catch it by going across the fields. The lilacs sighed their perfume over the walls of hidden gardens, and every heart remembered a summer that had been like this, a beautiful summer that would never come again.

The booths of the fair were lighted up on the square. Acrobats with expressionless faces turned easily around their bars, as if they were flying in a dream. A little chained black bear scattered sawdust as he ran about in his house of mirrors; and monkeys dressed in green and red costumes hitched a pair of dogs to a miniature cart. The whistle of the merry-go-round sounded, and you could set off on an intoxicating voyage that cost only a penny and that lasted just as long as a song. . . .

During September and October they went back
to stay at Elewyt. Winter came upon them in the
midst of the work and the pleasures of the country.
The first snow fell, and they were still there. Under every bush there was a fragile grotto of snow,
and the tracks of hares and birds crisscrossed over
the lawns.

"It is time to go back to town," said Mathilde.

After Christmas and New Year's had gone by,
it began to freeze. Barbara had some difficulty
standing up on her skates. "I don't know how to
skate any more. . . . I've forgotten," she exclaimed,
waving her arms to keep her balance. "Better hurry
up and learn!" said the other children. "St. Sylvain's Eve is not far off, and you must come to the
Ice Festival with us."

On St. Sylvain's Eve, in every house in the city, the children were given their dinner earlier than usual; then they were allowed to go out to skate in joyous companies. . . .

The sky was not very clear and it was barely freezing. Barbara was playing on the ice with her little friends. They were amusing themselves by cutting figures and circles, carrying lighted lamps. The moon came out from behind the clouds and made all the skates glitter.

"It is a rainy moon," said a lady, who had just arrived in a sleigh.

Barbara felt sad. Soon she knew why. Memories of the past year kept coming to her, and with them a wild hope. She understood that in her heart of hearts she had always hoped to find the ship again, in spite of what the little man in yellow had prophesied. Perhaps Jean des Brûlots had come back. Why shouldn't she go to the bend of the river and see? Surely he would not have forgotten her!

She separated from the children, and struck out northward, skating fast. The moon was hidden again. It was beginning to rain.

After the row of poplars at Zeel the ice was so grainy that skating became impossible.

Barbara made her way to the dike, climbed up it, clump-clump, and down again on the other side. Here she was in the small canal that ran along the dike on the opposite side from the river. The sur-

face of the ice seemed rather better. She had been skating for a long time when she saw two fishermen coming toward the city, striding along fast with their baskets of fish on their heads.

"The ice is breaking up," they called as they passed. "Spring is not far off. Watch out, little girl, or you'll get a wetting!"

Through the thick wall of the dike came dull sounds like distant explosions. Even in the canal the ice was now covered with water. Barbara realized that it was the beginning of the spring breakup. She felt afraid, and made her way to the bank.

Relieved to be on solid ground, she took off her skates, climbed the sloping embankment, and pushed on through the snow.

"Perhaps," she thought, "perhaps the ship will still be there. . . ."

She hurried along the tow-path, full of strength and hope. But she saw that everywhere the ice had cracked up under the push of the tide. The hoar frost was melting into the black water, icicles dropped into the current and were carried along.

And the ship had disappeared.

It had left those liberated waters, to return to the country of imagination and dreams.